CONTENTS

4

8

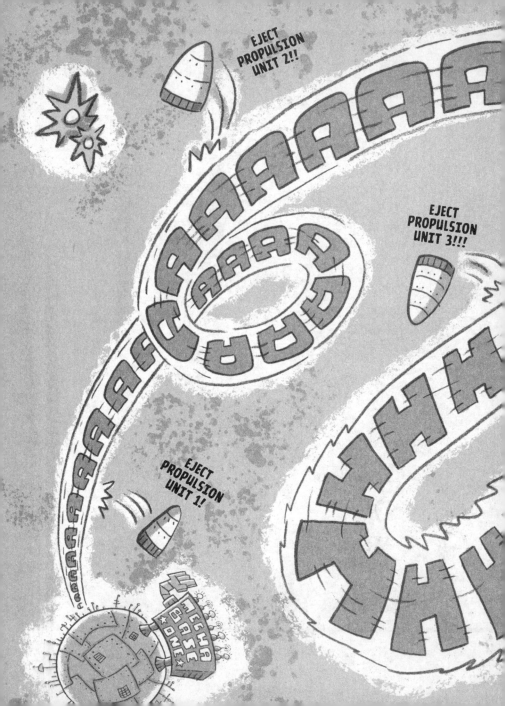

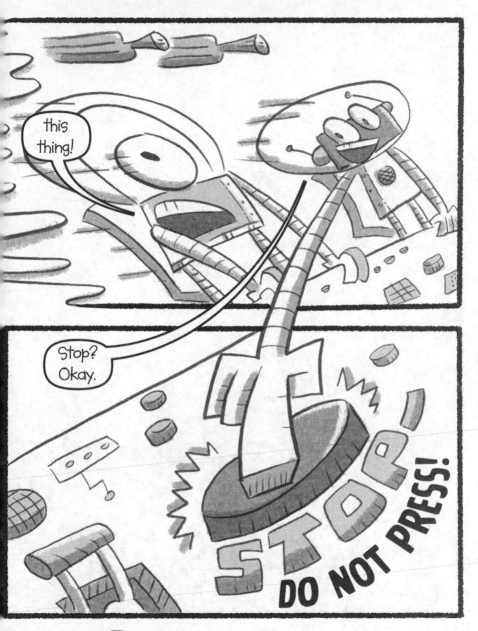

Let's find the space station before anyone else shows up.

Button Pusher

CHAPTER 6
Angry Aliens
Thank you for pressing the self-destruct button. The space station will blow up in ten minutes.
10:00
Why would anyone make a self-destruct button so big and put it out in the open? That's just bad planning!

WE TRAVEL FROM PLANET TO PLANET, SEARCHING FOR THE PERFECT PLACE TO CALL HOME.

WE FINALLY LANDED HERE AT THE SECRET SPACE STATION.

IT WAS PERFECT. THERE WAS ROOM TO STRETCH OUR TENTACLES.

IT WAS QUIET.

CONTACT SAGAN

IT WAS DARK. IT WAS COLD.

CHAPTER 7

Warning! Warning!

Hello, fellow humans! It is I, your friendly Bots host here to invite you on another adventure—WHOA! What are all these alarms? Why is everyone screaming? Where are we? Oh no, did this episode start without me?!

Hold on while I catch up.

Oh dear! The Bots need our help! We could build a rescue rocket to save them!

First we make a model rocket.

Then we build the real rocket.

Then we wait for the perfect day to launch the rocket.

Then we wait for the rocket to reach them, which takes a very long time because space is very big.

Then our rocket rescues them before the space station blows up!

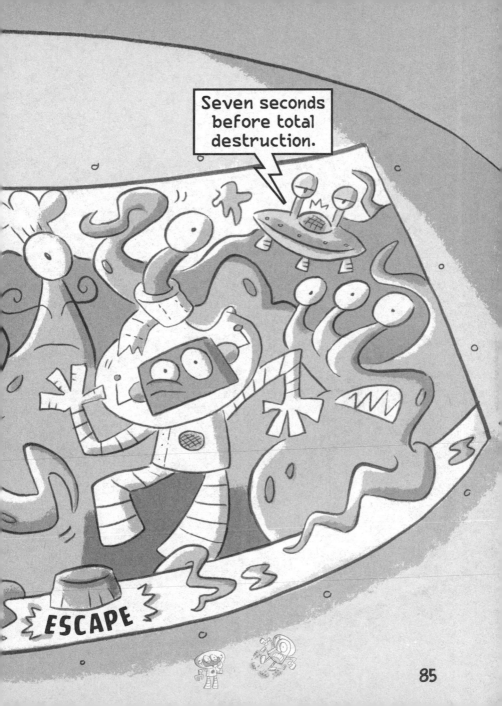

Invasion

I can't look! I can't look! Did they escape in time?

What? I can't hear you. Could you speak up?

A little louder.

A little louder.

Oh my, that was too loud! I hope you are not in a library or a crowded place because everyone will wonder why you are yelling at your book.

One Day Later

It's only been one day, and the Oozy Goozers have taken over every part of Mecha Base One.

They moved into the school.

They moved into the Mystery Tower.

They moved into the Robo-Ghost Town.

They moved into the beach under the sea.

They moved into Joe's extra bedroom.

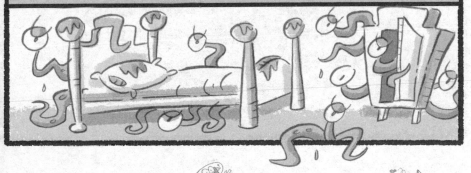

114

We take out the trash. Set the dinner table. Walk the cameras. Go to school all day. Mow the lawn. Take tests. Take baths and wash behind our antennas. Wear smelly sunscreen. Write essays. Do laundry. Load the dishwasher. Unload the dishwasher. Pick up dirty laundry. Set the breakfast table. Clean the bathroom. Rake leaves. Oh, and sometimes they don't let us have screen time.

CHAPTER 10

Bust a Move

Well, it looks like the Bots have their planet back thanks to grown-ups and rules.

123

TUNE IN NEXT TIME FOR...

by **Russ Bolts**   illustrated by **Jay Cooper**